SONIA NIMR grew up in Jenin, a small town in Palestine, then moved to England and took her doctorate in Oral History at the University of Exeter. After six years as an educational officer at the British Museum, she returned to Palestine to become head of the Museum Department at the Ministry of Tourism and Antiquities, and she now lectures in history and philosophy at Birzeit University. She is also a translator, has written a number of Palestinian folk tales for children, and together with Elizabeth Laird wrote the teenage novel *A Little Piece of Ground*. Sonia lives in Ramallah with her husband and son, where she loves reading, painting, jazz and old Arabic songs.

Ghaddar the Ghoul and other Palestinian Stories copyright © Frances Lincoln Limited 2007
Text copyright © Sonia Nimr 2007
Illustrations copyright © Hannah Shaw 2007

First published in Great Britain and in the USA in 2007 by
Frances Lincoln Children's Books, 4 Torriano Mews,
Torriano Avenue, London NW5 2RZ
www.franceslincoln.com

Distributed in the USA by Publishers Group West

British Library Cataloguing in Publication Data
available on request

ISBN: 978-184507-771-6

Printed in Singapore
1 3 5 7 9 8 6 4 2

Ghaddar the Ghoul

and other Palestinian Stories

Retold by Sonia Nimr
Illustrated by Hannah Shaw

Introduction by Ghada Karmi

F

FRANCES LINCOLN
CHILDREN'S BOOKS

For my son Kays, for the children of Palestine,
and for the children of the world – may you all strive to
make peace in this beautiful planet of ours

Contents

Introduction

Storytelling is an art and a part of life in Arab countries. It is no accident that the Tales from the Thousand and One Nights, though Persian in origin, should have become so popular in the Arabic-speaking world. Arabs grew up on tales of times past, of kings and wazirs and supernatural beings. Palestine, as a part of the Arab world, was no exception.

Traditionally, in every village or small town, there was a storyteller whose tales of past glories and legends drew large crowds. Tulkarm (in the West Bank), my family's town of origin, had a visiting storyteller who regularly held his audience spellbound with the skill of his narration. The name by which such men were known, hakawatis, was also used in a derogatory sense to mean someone who never stopped talking.

As a child in Jerusalem, I remember my mother telling us bedtime stories so exciting, they kept us awake rather than the reverse. Their recurring themes were of benevolent rulers, evildoers of various kinds (usually defeated by a combination of virtue, providence and magic), and happy endings. Jinn – which make an appearance in *Dancing Jasmine, Singing Water* – ghouls, animals, and inanimate objects imbued with magical powers, such as the golden saddle in *Hasan and the Golden Feather*, were other regular features of these stories, as familiar to us as if they were real.

When we fled our country in 1948 and ended up as refugees in London, my mother no longer told us stories. So I took over her role with my brother. Though younger than he, I had him spellbound with an epic tale I made up about a horrid ghoul relocated to North London, which I related in nightly, suspenseful instalments.

Sonia Nimr's wonderful collection of tales instantly evoked all those memories for me, as they will for others, and they will also introduce a new readership to the magical world of the Palestinian imagination. Place names here and there in the stories denote a Palestinian setting, but in fact many of the themes are common to other Arab stories. The humour, the ingenious plots and the magic in these tales will enchant readers.

Though originally told to grown-ups, who could divine their subtle social and political meanings, these stories retold by Sonia will enthrall children as much now as they once did my brother and me.

Ghada Karmi,
writer and broadcaster

Ghaddar the Ghoul

In the Valley of the Ghouls there lived a terrible, terrible ghoul. Once a year he would burst out of the valley and attack the surrounding towns, eating as many people as he could find before crashing back into the valley. His name was Ghaddar the Ghoul.

Then one year, Ghaddar attacked an entire city. Things were so bad that the king decided something must be done. So he made an announcement:

"Anyone who can bring me Ghaddar the Ghoul's three magic hairs shall marry my daughter and become king after me."

Now, everyone knew that Ghaddar's power lay in the three wiry hairs sprouting on his head, but no one dared to go near the Valley of the Ghouls, let alone try and pull out his hair. They had all seen the wall of human skulls surrounding the valley.

But there is always one person brave and crazy enough to try. In this city that person was Ahmad the Saddler. He decided to take his chances, so he said farewell to his family and his friends, not knowing if he would ever be back, and set out.

Ahmad walked for many days and many nights until he reached the valley. Climbing the wall of skulls, he entered a forest.

All at once, he heard a ghoul crying. The ghoul's cries were so loud that they made the trees shake and the earth tremble. Ahmad followed the sound, and saw a strange sight. The ghoul seemed to be stuck to a tree. His long, bushy hair was tangled around its branches.

When the ghoul saw Ahmad, he cried:

"If I wasn't caught in this tree, I'd eat you!"

But to the ghoul's surprise, Ahmad came closer. He raised his sword above his head and with mighty blows he cut the ghoul's hair and freed him.

The ghoul stood up, and Ahmad saw that his head barely reached the ghoul's knee!

"Thank you!" cried the ghoul. "If it wasn't for you, I would have been stuck to this tree for ever. But what brings you here, human?"

"I am looking for Ghaddar the Ghoul," replied Ahmad.

The ghoul was surprised. "What do you want him for?" he said.

"I want to take back his three magic hairs," declared Ahmed boldly.

The ghoul laughed.

"You want to take away the magic hairs from Ghaddar, King of the Ghouls? You must be crazy. Even we ghouls don't dare go near him."

But Ahmad was determined, so the ghoul said:

"You are a brave man; even I couldn't stop Ghaddar when he kidnapped my sister. I will tell you where to find him, and if you live – which I doubt – perhaps you can find out why my golden apple tree is dying.

The ghoul reached into his pocket, took a golden apple and gave it to Ahmad, saying, "If you see my sister, give her this apple and tell her we haven't forgotten her."

Ahmad thanked him and continued on his way deeper into ghoul-land. He climbed a high, rocky mountain, and when he reached the top he found a dried-up stream. There, beside the water, another ghoul was sitting. As Ahmad came nearer, he saw that this second ghoul was buried up to his knees in mud.

The ghoul called out:

"If I wasn't stuck in this mud, I'd eat you!"

Ahmad came closer, raised his sword, and to the ghoul's surprise he began to dig away the mud from around his legs. At last the ghoul could stand up and Ahmad saw that he was even bigger than the first one!

"Thank you!" said the second ghoul. "I see you've already met my brother." For the golden apple had fallen out of Ahmad's pocket while he was digging.

"What is a human like you doing in ghoul-land?" he asked.

"I'm looking for Ghaddar the Ghoul," replied Ahmad.

The second ghoul laughed.

"You must be out of your mind. He is the mightiest ghoul who ever lived. Even I couldn't stop him when he kidnapped my sister."

But Ahmad was determined to go on, so the ghoul

said, "You are a very brave human. I will tell you where to find him, and if you live – which I doubt – find out why my stream has dried up."

Then he pulled a ring from his finger and said, "If you see my sister, give her this ring and tell her we haven't forgotten her."

Ahmad took the ring, which was so big, he could wear it around his waist as a belt, and went on with his search.

✢ ✢ ✢

He walked for many days and nights, until he came to a lake. Another ghoul was fishing there. But when Ahmad came nearer, he saw that the ghoul's fingernails and toe-nails were so long and twisted that they had become entangled in the net.

The ghoul shouted:

"If my nails weren't caught in this net, I'd eat you!"

But Ahmad came closer, took out his big scissors and started to cut the ghoul's long, twisted nails, until finally he was free.

This third ghoul was even bigger than the previous two!

"Thank you!" he bawled.

Then he saw the ring around Ahmad's waist. He said, "Ah, I see you have met my brother. But what is a human doing in the Valley of the Ghouls?"

"I'm looking for Ghaddar the Ghoul," replied Ahmad.

The ghoul was surprised, and said, "Either you are mad, or you really want to die! Ghaddar is the strongest ghoul this valley has ever seen; even I couldn't stop him when he kidnapped my sister."

"But I must find him and take back the three magic hairs," said Ahmad.

"Then I will tell you where to find him," said the ghoul. "But if you live – which I doubt – find out why the fish are disappearing from my lake."

He gave Ahmad a small fish, and said, "If you see my sister, give her this and tell her we haven't forgotten her. But beware: if you find our sister grinding sugar, don't go near her. If you find her grinding salt, then you can approach her."

Ahmad thanked him and went on his way.

A few days later Ahmad found Ghaddar's house. He went inside and in the kitchen he saw a ghoula – Ghaddar's wife – grinding sugar. So he hid in a corner and watched her from a distance.

Suddenly a big snake slid into the room and was about to coil itself around her ankle – when the ghoula turned, to see Ahmad raising his sword. She gave a loud wail as Ahmad brought down the blade and struck off the snake's head.

The ghoula thanked him, and asked, "What are you doing here, human?"

Ahmad put the apple, the ring and the fish on the ground in front of her and said, "Your brothers have sent you these, to let you know that they haven't forgotten you."

The ghoula smiled at Ahmad, took her brothers' gifts and put them away. She was a terrible sight, with her long, tangled hair and dirty face, and Ahmad felt sorry for her. He offered to cut her hair and wash her face, and when he had finished, he took a mirror from his pocket and told her to look at herself.

The ghoula was very pleased, and said to him, "Thank you – but didn't you know that this is Ghaddar's house? If he finds you here, he will eat your flesh and crush your bones."

Ahmad said, "I've come here because I want to

take back Ghaddar's three magic hairs."

"That's impossible," said the ghoula. "Do you know how big and strong he is? Even my three brothers couldn't stop him when he kidnapped me."

As she spoke, the earth began to tremble. Ghaddar's thunderous footsteps were making the walls shake.

"You must hide!" said the ghoula. "If he sees you, you're dead!" And she hid Ahmad in the stable with the horses.

Next moment, Ghaddar crashed in through the door. He sniffed around, and roared, "I smell a human! Where is he?"

His wife replied, "There are no humans here. I haven't seen one since dinner last week. It must be the horses."

"No, it's a human smell – and whoever it is, I want them!"

"Maybe the smell is coming from your clothes," she said, and quickly changed the subject. "Do you like my hair?"

But Ghaddar was still sniffing around, so she said, "You look tired, Let me bring you dinner. I've made a special lamb stew for you with ten succulent lambs."

Ghaddar sat down to eat. He ate the flesh from all the lambs, crunched the bones and licked the plate clean. Then he was sleepy.

"Why don't you lie down and put your head on my lap," said the ghoula, "and I'll pick off the lice."

Then she asked, "Tell me, why is my brother's apple tree dying?" and she pulled a hair out of his head.

The ghoul was so sleepy, he didn't notice what she had done. He replied, "Because the fool hasn't noticed that there are rats eating the roots of his tree."

Then she asked, "Why is my brother's stream drying up?" and tweaked out another hair.

He replied, "Because alligators, frogs, turtles and other wretched animals drink straight from the spring where the stream begins."

She asked a third time, "Why are the fish disappearing from my brother's lake?" and pulled out the third hair.

He said sleepily, "Because there's a giant snake eating them. Now, enough questions. I want to sleep."

Soon he was snoring. The ghoula waited for a bit, then went to the stable. She gave Ahmad the three hairs, and said, "You must hurry. When he wakes, he will look for you. Tell my brothers I haven't forgotten them."

And she gave Ahmad the answers to her brothers' questions.

Ahmad started to make his way back. He found the third ghoul still trying to fish in his lake. The ghoul was surprised to see him and to hear what had happened to him.

When Ahmad told him why the fish were disappearing from his lake, the ghoul thanked him. "Go and dig under that fig tree. You will find a box," he said. "Take it."

Ahmad did as he said, and found the box, which was full of gold. Then he bade the ghoul farewell and continued on his way.

✤ ✤ ✤

Before long he met the second ghoul, who was just as surprised to see him.

"I thought you'd be dead!" he said.

Ahmad told him all that had happened at the ghoul's house and explained why his stream was drying up.

The ghoul thanked him and gave him a bag full of jewels.

✤ ✤ ✤

Ahmad continued on his way, until he met the first ghoul. "I never thought you'd make it," said the ghoul. "How did you defeat Ghaddar with that needle of yours?" – pointing to Ahmad's sword.

Ahmad replied, "I didn't defeat him with that. I defeated him with this –" and he pointed to his head. He told the ghoul what had happened and about his sister.

The ghoul asked, "Did you find out what is happening to my tree?"

Ahmad told him that rats were eating the roots. The ghoul thanked him, gave him an apple, and said, "If you ever need me, rub this apple three times."

20

Then he lifted Ahmad up on his back and flew him to the borders of the valley.

Ahmad returned to the city, gave the king all the gold and jewellery and showed him the three magical hairs.

The king kept his promise: Ahmad and the princess were married and the celebrations lasted for seven days and seven nights.

A few months later, Ghaddar's thunderous footsteps were heard once more approaching the city.

Ahmad waited outside the city wall, facing the ghoul as he approached.

He set light to one hair, and the ghoul howled in agony.

He burnt the second hair, and the ghoul fell screaming to the ground.

Then Ahmad shouted, "If you don't leave this city and never come back, I will burn the third hair and you will die!"

Ghaddar said craftily, "Give me the hair, and I will never come back."

"No," cried Ahmad. "This hair stays with me – and if ever again I hear that you have hurt anyone, I shall burn it!"

So Ghaddar the Ghoul left, never to return.

Rumour has it that he became a vegetarian.

The Farmer who Followed his Dream

In the village of Sirees there lived a farmer. He lived in a small house with two lemon trees in a garden at the front, where his wife grew vegetables and herbs. The farmer and his seven children worked all year round, but money was always short.

One morning, while they were having breakfast, his wife said, "You look worried. What is the matter?"

The farmer replied, "I had a dream last night, and I can't explain it. I dreamt that I had to go to Jerusalem – I don't know why – and I had to wait at a certain place by Damascus Gate."

"Wait for what?" asked his wife.

"That's it," said the farmer. "I have no idea what I was waiting for."

He went off to work, and by the end of the day he had forgotten all about his dream. But that night, and the night after that, he had the same dream again.

He said to his wife, "I've had the same dream for three nights. What do you think it means?"

His wife thought for a while, and said, "Why don't you go to Jerusalem, wait by Damascus Gate, and find out?"

So the farmer did. He bade his wife and children farewell, packed a few loaves of bread and some olives in his sack, and went on his way.

After walking for three days (he couldn't afford to hire a horse or a mule), he reached Damascus Gate in Jerusalem. There he stood and waited. People came and went, bought and sold, went to work and came back. Everyone passed by him, and still he waited. Some people even thought he was a beggar, and dropped a few coins on top of his sack.

The farmer waited and waited and waited, but nothing happened. Night came, shops closed, people went home, but still he waited. A stray dog watched him suspiciously and in the end it went off too, leaving the farmer alone and waiting.

Next day, the same thing happened.

On the third day he was still there.

On the third night, as the shops were closing, a man approached him, touched him gently on the shoulder, and said, "I own the leather shop just behind you, and I notice that you have been standing in the same spot for the last three days. What is your story?"

The farmer told the shopkeeper about his dream, "... and as you can see, I am still waiting for something to happen."

The shopkeeper laughed and laughed, and said, "That's the craziest thing I've ever heard. You walked for three days, and you waited here for three days and nights – just because of a dream?"

"Well, yes," the farmer said.

The shopkeeper laughed even more, and said, "Go home, my good man. You have already wasted six working days. Why? If everyone left their jobs to follow their dreams, no work would ever get done. Take me, for example. I had the same dream every

night for seven nights, and in the dream I saw treasure buried between two lemon trees in a garden in front of a small house in a village called Sss – see, I can't even remember the name! Do you really think I am crazy enough to close my shop and go to that godforsaken place to look for treasure I saw in a dream? I..."

But before the shopkeeper could finish, he saw to his surprise that the farmer had disappeared up the road out of sight...

Dancing Jasmine, Singing Water

Once there were three poor sisters who lived by making candles.

The king and his wazir happened to be walking in the streets, and they passed the hut where the young women lived. As they walked by, the king overheard one of the sisters saying, "If the king married me, I would bake him a cake big enough to feed the whole of his army."

The second said, even louder, "If the king married me, I would make him a candle big enough to light his entire palace."

The third cried, "And if the king married me, I would give him a son so brave that he could defeat an army all by himself, and a beautiful daughter with hair of silver and gold."

Next day, the king ordered the sisters to be brought to his palace. He asked the eldest sister to marry him and a few days later, commanded her to bake him a cake big enough to feed all his army. But the woman looked at him and said, "You must have been daydreaming. Did you really think I could bake such a big cake?"

This made the king very angry. He divorced the woman and sent her away. Then he married the second sister and a few days later, asked her to make him a candle big enough to light his entire palace. But she stared at him and said, "You must have been daydreaming. Did you really think I could make such a huge candle?"

The king grew even angrier. He divorced the woman and sent her away.

The king married the third sister and a few months later it was announced that his new queen was pregnant.

Her sisters grew insanely jealous, and when the queen gave birth to twins – a boy and a girl more beautiful than the sun and the moon – they made a bargain with the midwife. The midwife kidnapped the babies and put two little puppies in their place, telling the king that his wife had given birth to puppies.

The king was furious. He divorced his wife and sent her away. Then the two sisters told the midwife to put the babies in a basket and push it out into a nearby stream – and the basket floated away on the current.

A fisherman happened to be fishing further along

the stream and the basket got caught in his net. When he opened it, he found two babies as beautiful as the sun and the moon. He took the babies home to his wife and said, "Look, my dear, we have never had children – and now God has given us these!"

The fisherman's wife held the babies close. "They are a gift from God," she said. "We'll raise them as our own. But what shall we call them?"

The fisherman thought for a moment, and said, "Let's call the boy Shams (sun) and the girl Qamar (moon)."

✤ ✤ ✤

So the fisherman and his wife cared for the twins. The boy Shams grew to be a strong, brave young man, and his sister Qamar became a great beauty, with hair of gold and silver. She learnt to do the most exquisite embroidery. The children loved each other and were very close – so close that whenever Qamar was unhappy, it began to rain, and Shams knew that his sister was sad. When she was happy, the sun shone.

One day, years later, the fisherman said to the twins, "We have done the best we can for you, but now my wife and I are getting old. When we die, take the money we have saved and start a new life." And he told them that they were not his own children, but had been found in a basket floating downstream.

When eventually the fisherman and his wife died, Shams and Qamar decided to start a new life together. They wandered for a time, until one day they reached a big city, where they decided to live. Qamar started to embroider exquisite dresses for wealthy women, and Shams found a job with a merchant, becoming so successful that he built a splendid palace for himself and his sister.

Shams' reputation spread throughout the city and beyond. Even the king became a customer of his. The more the king dealt with Shams, the more he liked his honesty and his intelligence. Soon the two were great friends, and the king often sought Shams' advice on matters of state.

When the jealous aunts heard of the merchant who had became the king's friend, and of his gold- and silver-haired sister with magic hands, they realised at once that these must be their sister's children. And they decided to get rid of them.

They started to visit Qamar, pretending that they wanted to order embroidery. Qamar never suspected them for a moment.

One day, one of them said to her, "Your home is beautiful, but it still needs one thing to be perfect."

Qamar asked, "And what is that?"

Her aunt said, "It needs the Dancing Jasmine Tree. The tree spreads scent everywhere every time it dances." And she gave her sister a meaningful look.

Her sister said, "I wonder that your loving brother can deny you such a simple thing."

Hearing this, Qamar became sad and started to cry. Rain began to fall, and over the other side of the city, Shams at once knew that his sister was unhappy. He ran home and asked Qamar what was the matter.

She said, between sobs, "I am sad because our palace lacks something, and I can't live with the shameful knowledge that my brother, the only person who loves me in this world, has not given it to me."

"But what is missing, beloved sister?"

She said, "The Dancing Jasmine Tree – the one which spreads scent everywhere every time it dances."

Shams said, "If it pleases you, I will search for this tree and bring it back."

Shams travelled far and wide searching for the Dancing Jasmine Tree, but no one knew where it could be found. Then one day he was resting in a field under a fig tree, when suddenly he saw a small snake slithering away, pursued by a python.

Shams raised his sword and quickly killed the python.

The small snake came up to him, curled herself near his feet, and said, "Thank you for saving my life. How can I be of service?"

Shams laughed. "How can a snake help me?"

The snake reared up, shook herself – and turned into a woman!

"I am from the Land of Jinn. I took the form of a snake to escape from that ugly python jinn who wanted to marry me."

Shams asked her about the Dancing Jasmine Tree. The jinn told him, "That tree is far, far away. It would take you at least three years to get there and another three to come back. Besides, the jasmine garden is guarded by a terrible ghoul."

But Shams was determined to go, so the jinn disappeared and returned with a male jinn. She said to Shams, "This is my brother Asif. He will take you there in three minutes. But beware of the ghoul. If you find him awake, say '*Al salam 'Alikum*' and you will be safe. If you find him asleep, don't go near him. Farewell, my friend!"

Three minutes later, Shams was standing in the jasmine garden. Suddenly he heard footsteps shaking the ground, and a voice roared out, "Who dares to enter my garden?"

A giant ghoul approached. His eyes were red, his nose was long and twisted, his hair straggled down to the ground.

Shams cried, "*Al salam 'Alikum*, O Mighty Ghoul, Guardian of the Garden!"

The ghoul's hideous features softened a little, and he said, "If it wasn't for your *salam*, I would have devoured you. What do you want?"

Shams said, "I want a jasmine tree which dances and spreads its scent everywhere."

"What do you want it for?" asked the ghoul.

Shams said, "For my sister."

The ghoul said wistfully, "I had a sister once." And he bent his long torso and pulled out one of the trees, gave it to Shams, and said, "Here, give this to your sister and make her happy."

Shams thanked him, mounted on the jinn's back and flew home. He planted the tree in the middle of the garden and watched it with Qamar as it began to move and dance, sending the scent of jasmine everywhere.

A few days later, the two sisters visited Qamar, saw the Dancing Jasmine Tree and knew that Shams hadn't died as they had hoped.

One of the sisters said, "That is the most beautiful jasmine tree I have ever seen. Your palace is almost perfect – but alas, it still lacks one thing."

She looked at her sister, who said, "Your brother gave you all these things, yet he denies you the one thing which would make your palace perfect."

Qamar asked, "And what is that?"

The two sisters replied, "The Singing Water, of course – the water which sings the most beautiful tunes when it flows in the fountain."

This left Qamar feeling sad.

When Shams saw that it was pouring with rain, he knew something was wrong and ran home to find Qamar in tears. He asked what was the matter, and she said:

"I am sad because our palace lacks something, and I can't live with the shameful knowledge that my brother, the only person who loves me in this world, hasn't given it to me."

Shams asked, "What is this thing, my beloved sister?"

She said, "It is the Singing Water which makes the most beautiful tunes when it flows into the fountain."

Shams said, "If it pleases you, I will search for it and bring it back."

✥ ✥ ✥

Shams searched for the Singing Water, but no one knew where to find it. He travelled for many days until he found himself near the same fig tree where he had met the jinn. He called her – and she came.

She asked him, "What brings you back? Didn't you find the Jasmine Tree?"

Shams replied, "Yes, but now I'm looking for the Singing Water."

The jinn said, "The singing water is in a fountain guarded by a monstrous ghoula, and she doesn't respond to the words *Al salam 'Alikum*".

Then she took pity on Shams, and said,

"The ghoula has one weakness: she loves honey – but the honey must come from the beehive on the White Mountain. It will take you five years to get there and another five to come back – if you manage to climb up the mountain's slippery side."

When he heard this, Shams was dismayed, but he said, "I must go there."

"I will ask my brother Kasir to take you," said the jinn, "but you will have to climb the mountain on your own, because we are not allowed there." And she summoned her brother.

Shams thanked her, mounted Kasir's back and off they flew. They landed at the foot of the White Mountain.

"This is as far as I can take you," said Kasir. "When you come back – if you come back – you'll find me waiting here."

Shams started to climb the mountain, but the surface was steep and slippery and for every step he took, he fell back two. He used his sword, his ropes and every bit of his strength until finally he reached the summit. There he found a giant beehive. Covering himself with his cloak, he approached it cautiously, filled a jar with honey and climbed carefully down again, to find Kasir waiting for him.

Off they flew to the fountain with singing water.

Shams was about to fill his water jar when he heard the ghoula approaching.

She roared, "Who dares to steal water from my fountain?"

Shams thrust out the jar of honey and said, "I've brought you a gift of friendship."

The ghoula took the jar and swallowed the honey in one gulp. Then she smiled and said, "If it weren't for your gift, I would have eaten you alive." And she allowed him to fill his water jar.

Shams went home and built a beautiful fountain for Qamar. When he poured in the water, it began to sing.

But when his two aunts came to visit Qamar and heard the singing water, they knew that their plan hadn't worked.

"What a wonderful fountain!" they cried, "Listen to the water! Your palace is almost perfect, but alas, it still lacks one thing to make it perfect."

"And what is that?" asked Qamar.

"The Wise Bird," they replied. "You can't have Singing Water and a Dancing Tree without having the Wise Bird too. Your brother has bought you everything, and yet he denies you the one thing which would make your palace perfect."

Qamar started to cry, and when Shams came,

she told him about the Wise Bird.

⁜ ⁜ ⁜

Shams set out to find the bird. When he reached the fig tree, the jinn came out to meet him.

"What is it this time?" she cried.

"I'm searching for the Wise Bird," replied Shams.

"That bird is found in the Land of Weeping Willows," said the jinn, "and whoever hears their weeping will go mad."

"But I must go there," Sham said.

"I will ask Rabid to take you there," said the jinn. And she summoned her brother.

Shams mounted Rabid's back and they flew to the Land of Weeping Willows. When they arrived, the sound of weeping was deafening, and Shams felt a terrible sadness invade his heart. But before it could drive him mad, he poured some water on the ground, mixed it into mud and stuffed it into his ears to block out the noise. Then he spotted the Wise Bird, caught hold of it and put it in the cage he'd brought with him.

He went home, opened the cage door, and the bird hopped out on to his wrist. Then he put it into the Dancing Tree.

As soon as the bird settled, it began to sing:

> "*The King had children,*
> *a daughter and a son.*
> *The King has children:*
> *the Moon and the Sun!*"

Shams and Qamar didn't understand what the bird was saying and thought it was just singing its song. But the bird kept repeating the words over and over again.

One day, the king came to visit Shams and Qamar. They sat in the garden and the king was amazed to see the Dancing Tree and to hear the Singing Water in the fountain.

Suddenly the wise bird began to sing,

> "*The King had children,*
> *a daughter and a son.*
> *The King has children:*
> *the Moon and the Sun!*"

When he heard this, the king looked hard at Shams and Qamar, and suddenly realised who they were. Tears poured down his cheeks as he hugged his children and told them about their mother. Then he rushed back to the palace, ordered the midwife to be found and made her tell him the truth. Realising that he had done his third wife a great wrong, the king brought her back and apologised. The family was together again!

As for the two wicked aunts, the king wanted to have them burnt at the stake, but the queen pleaded for her sisters' lives. So the king was merciful – and banished them for ever.

Tanbouri's Clown

From the first day I saw Tanbouri, my life has been a hard one. I took him everywhere. He walked me on hard grounds, wet puddles and slippery tiles. He used me as a hammer. He squashed little insects with me. He never spent a single penny looking after me, and he didn't even bother to clean me. Did I complain? No. I kept my mouth shut, hoping that one day he would tire of me and put me into retirement.

But no, my rich, miserly owner went on using me, over and over and over again, until one day I woke up and couldn't remember what my original colour had been.

You are probably wondering who I am. I thought you knew! I am Tanbouri's old shoes. I shall tell you my story from the very beginning, so you won't think that I'm just a moaner.

The cobbler made me a work of art. People came from all over the city just to admire my beautiful design and colour, which changes in the sun from red to brown. I was hoping a king would buy me, or a prince, or a rich merchant who appreciates art.

44

But no, as fate would have it, I was bought by a perfume-maker. "Oh well," I thought, "a perfume-maker is sure to appreciate a piece of work like me."

No such luck.

As the years passed, Tanbouri wore me out, leaving me patched, with ugly stitches showing. I was falling apart at the seams. I became the laughing-stock of the city. They called me 'Tanbouri's clown'.

But did Tanbouri care? Not a jot.

One day Tanbouri went to Friday prayers. He met his friend, who gave me a long, hard stare and said to him, "My dear friend, why don't you give those old shoes a rest? Buy yourself a new pair. It is not good for a man in your position to be seen wearing them. I'll tell you what: I will buy you some new shoes." (Everyone knew that Tanbouri was a miser.)

They went inside the mosque to pray, and I was left with the rest of the shoes. You can't believe the humiliation I felt, with all those nice, clean shoes staring at me.

Prayers over, the men came out, put on their shoes

and left. Eventually there were two pairs left, me and a beautiful pair with golden shoe-laces gleaming in the sun. Tanbouri assumed that the nice shoes were the gift promised earlier by his friend. He put them on and home he went.

When a judge came out looking for his shoes, all he could find was me. Of course, he knew at once whose shoes I was (see – I told you I was famous!). Since he couldn't find anything else to wear, the judge put me on and hurried home, hoping that no one would see him.

Next day, imagine how proud I felt to be seated beside the judge in the big lofty court! The judge ordered Tanbouri to be brought in. I needn't tell you what colour Tanbouri's face went when he was ordered to pay a fine of one hundred gold pieces. He decided then and there to get rid of me.

He put me outside his gate beside the garbage bin, thinking the garbage man would take me away. But the man said, "Poor Tanbouri, he must have forgotten all about his beloved shoes." So he put me inside the gate where Tanbouri would see me when he got home.

After that, Tanbouri took me to the river, dumped me there and went back home. I found myself caught up in the current, which carried me towards the city

sewer. Well, I couldn't help blocking it, could I? *Pooh!* You wouldn't believe the stink. When the judge was told that I was the cause of the blockage, Tanbouri was hauled back into the court and fined another hundred gold pieces.

Tanbouri was furious. He sat and thought for a while, then took me up on the roof, lit a fire, and threw me on it. "Burn, you wretches!" he cried. A thick, black smoke rose from the roof and darkened the sky.

The judge happened to be asthmatic. It took his doctors two hours to stop him coughing.

The next day, when Tanbouri was brought before the judge, he knew the sentence would be harsh – and it was: fifty lashes and a hundred more gold pieces.

Tanbouri was distraught. He had to get rid of me. He sat up that night jotting down ideas, until at last – "Eureka!" he shouted, waking me from a nice dream.

Next morning, he took his boat out to sea. There, in the middle of nowhere, he dropped me, and I hit the water with a splash. Then he sailed back to shore.

The last thought I had before I sank was, "Praise be to Allah! I'm retired at last!" But before I could explore my last resting-place, I was swept up out of the water into a huge net.

When the fisherman saw me, he shouted,

"It's Tanbouri's shoes!" He took me out of his net and laid me out to dry. The poor man thought that if he took me back to my owner, he would be rewarded.

So here I was at Tanbouri's gate again, in the hands of the fisherman. He knocked on the door, but Tanbouri was not at home so he waited for a while. Just as he was about to leave, he noticed an open window on the top floor. The fisherman threw me in through the window, then went home.

You should have seen Tanbouri's face when he got home and saw the mess! There was broken glass everywhere and streams of perfume running across the floor. Poor Tanbouri! Out of one disaster straight into another! When he saw me and realised this was all my fault, his face changed colour and he started pulling out his hair and began to curse. I swear I saw his mouth growing fangs and his hands sprouting claws. He grabbed me and marched straight up on to the roof. Then he hurled me over the edge with all his might.

"*Ahhhhhh!*" What on earth was that? I had hit someone hard on the head. That poor judge just happened to be walking down below, never expecting a pair of shoes to fall from the sky. You never heard such a crack, not to mention the big red lump which swelled up on his bald head.

This time, people came to the trial from miles around. Schools closed, shops shut their doors, and the streets were full of people pushing and shoving to hear what the verdict would be. Everyone thought that this time the judge would show no mercy.

The tension mounted as Tanbouri was brought in, chained hand and foot. Everyone strained forward and held their breath. There was utter silence.

The judge touched the lump on his head. Tanbouri thought, "That's it. I've had it. I'm dead."

Suddenly… "*Ha ha! Ha-ha-ha!*" To everyone's surprise, the judge started to laugh. He laughed and laughed until the tears ran down his cheeks. People thought his brain had been affected by the accident.

Then he spoke.

"Tanbouri, I can't take any more of this. You've nearly killed me twice, and you've lost a lot of money – all because you are so stingy. Why don't I take these wretched shoes of yours? I'm sure I can put them to good use. As for you, this time there will be no prison, no lashes and no fine either. I think you've learned your lesson."

Tanbouri certainly learnt his lesson; now he buys

new shoes every month.

As for me, I finally retired and – would you believe it? – ended up as a famous landmark. They put me on a plinth in the market square, with my story inscribed in gold letters for all to read!

How Swallow Tricked Snake

Once upon a time, long, long ago, the Devil was kicked out of Paradise because he was so bad.

At once he started thinking of ways to get back in. He sat outside for a while, looking sad. Then he talked to the animals around him, to see who would help.

As soon as he saw Snake, he thought he might be in luck.

Snake listened to the Devil as he told him his plan:

"I know that everything's easy for you, Snake, so why don't I sit on your tooth and you just carry me in. No problem, no mess."

Snake thought for a bit, and finally said yes.

Now, if you want to know why Snake agreed, the simple answer is – greed. The Devil promised Snake a very tasty reward. Once Snake got back into Paradise, he promised her that she would eat human flesh for ever and ever. He told Snake, "Human flesh is better than honey or milk. It slips down your throat more softly than silk."

Snake did exactly as she was told, and the Devil sneaked back into Paradise.

Pretty soon, Snake wanted her reward. She went to the Devil and said, "You've got what you wanted. Now I want what you promised."

The Devil said, "Have it. It's yours – you deserve it." Snake snapped her jaws with excitement, thinking about her tasty meal to come.

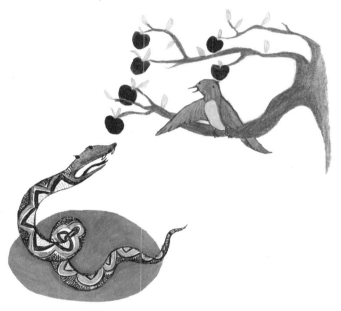

But Swallow, who was a clever bird, was flying nearby and overheard the conversation. Now, Swallow was a good friend to Adam and Eve. She wasn't going to let Snake have them for supper. So she smoothly asked Snake, "Are you sure human flesh is the best meat to eat?"

"That's what the Devil told me," said greedy Snake.

"But who can believe what the Devil says?" asked Swallow. "Every time he opens his mouth, lies tumble out." She thought for a moment. "I know – let's send Mosquito to scout round the world and taste each animal one by one. She can come back when the year is out and let us all know if humans really do taste best."

Snake thought for a moment, then nodded and said, "You're right – it's the only way to find out."

And she turned to Mosquito, "Off you go, now!"

Mosquito took off around the world and began to taste all kinds of meat.

Up high mountains, across wide seas, over golden deserts, through green trees.

Sun and rain, floods and snow, nothing made Mosquito slow.

She tasted every animal big and small – a bite of each, she tried them all.

Mosquito was so busy tasting, she didn't notice that Swallow was following her and never let her out of her sight.

The year passed quickly, and soon it was time for the animals to gather again. Everyone was waiting for Mosquito's report – most of all Swallow, who was anxious about the fate of her human friends.

She was so worried, she flew up and overtook Mosquito.

"Please, please, I'm dying to know, which meat will be the snake's prize?" she asked. "Come on, do tell – we can share the surprise."

Mosquito said, "OK, I'll tell you. Devil was right: human meat really is the very, very best."

"I'm sorry," said Swallow, moving closer. "I didn't hear. I'm going deaf in my right ear."

Mosquito breathed in, breathed out – to make Swallow hear, she had to shout! She opened her mouth as wide as she could – and quick as a flash Swallow got her tongue.

"*Bzzzz*," said Mosquito. "*Bzzz, bzzz, bzzz –*" but no words came out.

"Don't worry," said Swallow. "I'll tell the animals what you were going to say."

Everyone was waiting for Mosquito. But no one minded Swallow telling them the news – they'd all seen her flying behind Mosquito. They crowded round, and she said:

> "I know the answer.
> Mosquito told me before she lost her voice:
> Frog meat, she said – that was her choice,
> That's what Mosquito liked the best.
> She tasted everything, but didn't like the rest."

Snake was furious.
She knew it was
a trick, and said to
Swallow, "I'll get
you for this." And before anyone
could stop her, Snake took a bite at
Swallow's tail. She got a mouthful of feathers,
and Swallow started to wail. She'd been paid back
with a fork in her tail!

Snake smacked her lips. She was all ready to
crunch frog meat for lunch.

So now you know why mosquitoes can't speak, why
snakes eat frogs, and why swallows have forked tails!

I Landed at the Prince's Party

Long, long ago in the land of Palestine, there lived a mighty king. His kingdom was vast, his lands were fertile and his riches couldn't be counted. His people loved him because he was just and kind.

The king had a son who was brave and wise and who loved reading. The king wanted his son to marry, but each time the subject came up, the prince would say that he hadn't found the right woman.

One day, the king said to his son, "There are many princesses in my kingdom. Why don't you choose one of them to be your wife?"

The prince replied, "The woman of my dreams doesn't have to be a princess."

The king said, "Then choose from one of our rich, noble families."

The prince answered, "She doesn't have to be rich or from a noble family."

"Then choose the most beautiful woman in the kingdom," insisted the king.

"She doesn't have to be beautiful," said the prince stubbornly.

The king was beginning to lose his patience. "Then who is the woman of your dreams?"

"She must be clever, smart and know how to tell stories," the prince said.

"How are we going to find such a woman?" asked the king doubtfully.

"Easy," said the prince. "We'll have a party and invite all the young women in the land, and the one who can tell a story that begins and ends with lies – the one who makes me smile – shall be my wife."

Invitations were sent out, and preparations for the party began.

The big day came, and young women from every part of the kingdom flocked to the palace, each wearing her best clothes and each dreaming of becoming the prince's wife.

The storytelling began.

A princess came forward. Her dress was of the finest silk, her hair was braided with golden thread and her jewellery shone in the candlelight. She was beautiful as a rose and graceful as a swan. With a voice like the gentle flow of a river, she began her story:

"Once upon a time, there –" but before she could go on, the prince stopped her with a gesture of his hand and said, "All stories begin like that. I want a story that begins and ends with lies."

One by one, the other women began to tell their stories, but none managed to impress the prince.

The prince looked bored and was about to leave the party, when a young woman came forward. She was plainly dressed, and her long black hair was arranged in simple braids. With the most spectacular smile the prince had ever seen, she sat in front of him and, without waiting for an introduction, she began:

"When my grandparents first married, I was invited to their wedding."

Everyone in the great hall fell silent, and the prince smiled for the first time that evening.

"They gave me an egg as a wedding present. It was as big as a watermelon, white as a full moon on a summer night and smooth as the cheek of a baby. I played with it on the way home, throwing it from one hand to the other. But suddenly it fell on the ground and broke into two halves. Out of my egg came a huge rooster. It was as colourful as the meadows in the spring, and as big and strong as a horse. I said to myself, 'Oh well, since it is so big, I can ride it like a horse.'

"On the back of my rooster I travelled everywhere – through forests, rivers, seas and valleys, over islands, mountains, cities and faraway lands. I was enjoying myself so much that I didn't notice that the back of my rooster was becoming infected.

"I went to the medicine man and asked for a cure. He said, 'Take the stone of a date and crush it at noon. Then, when the moon is full, spread the date oil on the rooster's back. By morning he will be better.'

"I did exactly what he told me. Next morning, I went to check on my rooster and lo and behold, a huge palm tree had grown up on his back!"

Everybody in the hall was holding their breath.

"On the top of the palm tree were the biggest, brownest, juiciest dates I had ever seen. I started throwing stones at the top of the tree and the dates began to fall down. I ate ninety-nine dates very slowly, savouring the taste. The hundredth I ate very quickly, as a thought suddenly came into my mind. The stones, which I threw at the top of the tree, hadn't come down. So I decided to climb the tree and find out why.

"I was still climbing the tree when the sun went down, so I slept the night on a branch using pieces of bark as cover. I continued to climb the next day and reached the top of the tree before the sun went down.

"I rubbed my eyes with disbelief. For there, stretched out in front of my eyes, was the largest and most fertile land I had ever seen.

"'*Yehhhhhh*,' I cried. 'This is my land on top of my tree, which grew on the back of my rooster, which came out of my egg!'

"I began to think, what shall I grow on my land? I decided to grow sesame seeds. In the morning I planted the seeds, in the afternoon the harvest was ready and I started to gather the harvest. I filled thousands of sacks with thousands of kilos of sesame seeds.

"When I had finished, I counted my seeds and found that one was missing. Who had taken my sesame seed? I looked around and saw an ant running away with it. I ran after the ant and took hold of my sesame seed, but the ant was holding tightly on to the other end. So I pulled, and the ant pulled, I pulled, and the ant pulled – until the seed was broken and a sea of sesame oil burst out of it.

"*Hurrrrrrrah!* Instead of one, now I had two harvests!

"I began to think what I should plant next. I decided to grow watermelons. I planted the seeds in the morning, and in the afternoon the harvest was ready and my watermelons were ripe.

"I was collecting my watermelons when I noticed a giant square, blue watermelon at the far end of my field. Thinking this would be the juiciest and tastiest of all, I pulled out my twenty-metre sword and made a square cut into the giant melon. But just as I was putting a piece of the fruit into my mouth, I noticed a stairwell in my melon. I decided to investigate, so I climbed down the stairs to the bottom. There I found a market place, with people coming and going, buying and selling goods of all sorts – meats, vegetables, brass pans, pottery jars, leather, books and many other things.

"As I was wandering around, I saw an old man sitting on the ground looking sad. I asked him what the matter was. The old man pointed to his donkey, which was lying on its back with one leg crossed over the other, one foreleg under its head and the other holding a pipe with smoke drifting out of it. The old man said that his donkey was refusing to move, and that he had many deliveries to make. I wanted to help, so I told the man to hold the donkey's head while I held its tail, and together we would make him stand upright.

"One, two, three, pull! But the donkey did not move.

"One, two three, pull! But still the donkey would not move.

"One, two, three, pu – the donkey's tail came off in my hand!

"When the old man saw what had happened, he started to shout and wave his arms about. His shouting attracted a big crowd out of nowhere, and he demanded justice.

"I was arrested and taken to jail. On the day of the trial, everybody was suggesting suitable punishments for me. The judge was still considering his verdict when someone came up with an ingenious idea. 'Let's banish the stranger.' 'Yes, yes!' the others shouted.

'Let's put the stranger in the barrel of a cannon and shoot her away!'

"The next day, everyone gathered to watch as I was squeezed into the barrel of a cannon. When I was shot into the air, I heard them cheer. Above the clouds I flew, up with the birds, and I rode on a rainbow. I saw the mountains below me and the people beneath as small as ants. I flew and flew, until I landed – at the prince's party!"

The prince laughed out loud and clapped his hands. He had finally found the woman with whom he would spend the rest of his life.

Hungry Wolf and Crafty Fox

nce there was a hungry wolf. He searched everywhere for food but he couldn't find any. As he roamed the fields looking for something to eat, he met a shepherd looking after his sheep. The wolf saw the big fat lambs and felt even hungrier, but he couldn't get near them because of the shepherd.

Wolf decided to play a trick on the shepherd, so he went to him and said, "Good morning, my good Shepherd."

The shepherd replied, "Good morning to you, Wolf. What brings you so far from your home?"

Wolf replied, "I came to see how fat my two lambs are – you know, the two I gave you to fatten up for me."

The shepherd was puzzled and asked, "Which two lambs do you mean?"

Wolf smiled a wicked smile, showing all his sharp teeth, and said, "Have you forgotten? I gave you two small lambs last year and asked you to fatten them up for me. Now I'd like them back."

The shepherd suspected that the wolf was lying,

so he said, "I'm a new shepherd here, and I know nothing about them."

Wolf insisted: "I want my lambs now!"

"But," said the shepherd, "how do I know if you gave two lambs to the shepherd before me? Are you willing to swear on the Cross at the shrine of Al Khadir – whom Christians call Saint George – that the lambs are yours? And beware of lying, because anyone who swears a false oath at the shrine is sure to be punished."

Wolf thought for a moment, then decided to ask his friend Fox for advice.

He went to Fox, told him his story and asked him what he thought.

Fox, imagining the succulent taste of fresh lamb, said, "People say that if you swear a false oath on the shrine of Al Khadir, punishment will fall on the son of the son of your son."

"Well," said Wolf, "I'm very hungry, and since the punishment will fall on my descendants and not on me, I'll risk it."

So he went back and told the shepherd he was ready to take the oath.

"Then," said the shepherd, "meet me there at dusk."

When the sun set, Wolf met the shepherd at the shrine, and there he saw two big lambs tied at the foot of a large oak tree. Two enormous dogs were also there, lying asleep.

"First," said the shepherd, "you must put your paw on the Cross on top of the shrine and swear the oath, then you must climb up the tree and shout from the top branch that the two lambs are yours. If you are telling the truth, fine – but if you are lying, you'll be punished!"

Wolf put his paw on the Cross and swore the oath, then climbed the tree, and when he reached the top branch, swore the oath again at the top of his voice.

His howling woke the dogs, who started barking – and the barking startled Wolf so much that he lost his balance and fell out of the tree, injuring a leg – and barely escaped from the vicious dogs waiting below.

Some weeks later, when Wolf was feeling better, he went to find Fox. He said angrily, "You told me that it's always the descendants of liars who get punished. So why did I get punished right away?"

Fox replied, "Ah, that was punishment for what your father's father's father did. It had nothing to do with you at all!"

Stupid Salma

here was a merchant living in a village near Jerusalem. He was married to a woman named Salma.

One day, after the merchant had gone to work, Salma heard a street vendor shouting, "I sell names! Beautiful new names!"

Salma called him in and asked, "Did you say you sell new names?"

The vendor replied, "Yes, my lady, I sell brand new names. What is the name of the beautiful lady I see standing before me?"

"My name is Salma."

The vendor looked sad and said to her, "Dear, oh dear! How could such a sweet, pretty woman as you have such an ugly name?"

Salma, who wasn't very bright, said, "Well, I'm not very happy with it either. Have you a better name for me?"

"Of course. And I won't even bother to charge you. I will give you a name worthy of a queen, and in return I will take anything – an old jar, a bowl, a pot – anything. You will never find such a bargain anywhere."

Salma grew very excited. Not only was she going to have a new name, but it would cost her almost nothing! She went in, brought out an old pottery jar,

and said, "Well? What name have you for me?"

The vendor put the jar in a sack hanging from his donkey's saddle. He looked at Salma with a big smile and said, "From now on, you are Salloma! Goodbye to ugly Salma, welcome to beautiful new Salloma!"

With that, he jumped on the back of his donkey and was gone in a flash.

When the merchant came home from work, he called his wife. "Salma! Salma! Where are you?"

But there was no answer. He looked all through the house and finally found her standing in the middle of the kitchen with a big grin on her face.

"Salma, I have been calling you for ages. Why didn't you answer me?"

She looked at him and said, "That's because I am no longer Salma. Today I got a new name: from now on I am Salloma. Isn't it lovely? I bought it for almost nothing – just the old pottery jar we had in the attic."

The merchant couldn't believe his ears. "Did you say the old jar in the attic?"

"Yes – isn't it marvellous? Isn't it a bargain?"

The merchant was speechless. His face turned red, then green, then grey.

"What have you done, woman?"

Salloma was surprised.

"Why are you so angry? It's only a name."

"It's not the name, you fool. It's the jar. All my life's savings were hidden in that jar."

"Oh, I hadn't thought of that," said Salloma.

"It's no good. I can't live with such a stupid woman," said the merchant. "I am going away, and only if I find someone who is more stupid than you will I ever come back."

And with that, he left home and began his search.

✛ ✛ ✛

One day, he came to a small village. There was a celebration, a wedding procession, and the bride was being escorted on a horse. But the men around her were arguing and shouting.

The merchant went closer to find out what was going on. He heard one of the men saying, "That arch over the gate is too low. We must find a way to get the bride into the yard."

Another man said, "I say we cut off the horse's legs."

Another said, "Do you know how much I paid for that horse?"

And another: "I say we demolish the arch."

Yet another shouted, "I worked two months to build that arch. You'll have to think of something else."

Then a man came forward and said, "I say we cut off the bride's head."

A man answered, "I'm not letting you cut off my daughter's head!"

And so the argument continued.

The merchant couldn't believe what he was

hearing. He raised his hands and shouted, "I have a solution!"

The men all stopped shouting and looked at him. The merchant went up to the bride and said to her, "Lower your head, and lean forward."

The bride did as he told her, and she passed through the gate easily.

Everyone fell silent. "We hadn't thought of that," they mumbled.

✚ ✚ ✚

The merchant continued on his way. A few days later he came to another village. He saw a group of people arguing, went closer to find out what the matter was, and saw a boy with his hand stuck in a jar.

One of the men was saying, "I say we break the jar."

Another said, "No, I won't let you break my jar."

Another man said, "Why not cut off the boy's hand?"

And another: "I'm not letting you cut off my boy's hand!"

The merchant looked closely at the boy's hand and asked, "What are you holding in your hand?"

"Three eggs," the boy replied.

"Put the eggs down and take out your hand," said the merchant.

The boy did as he was told, and his hand came out easily. Everyone was so surprised! Then the merchant told the boy to put his hand inside the jar again and to take out one egg... then another... and then a third, until there was a small pile of eggs on the ground.

The men looked at the merchant respectfully and said, "We hadn't thought of that!"

✣ ✣ ✣

The merchant continued his journey. He travelled many days and many nights, until finally he came to a village. There he found a group of men standing around a carpet arguing.

One man was saying, "As the richest of the four families in this village, my family should carry the king's gift to the mosque."

Another said, "No. We are the oldest of the four families and we should carry the carpet to the mosque."

Another one said, "But my family is the biggest."

And another: "The imam comes from my family, so we should carry it."

Then a man came forward and said, "I say we cut the carpet into four pieces and each family can carry a piece."

Another said, "We can't cut up a gift from the king. I say we hold a duel and the victorious family can have the honour of carrying the carpet."

The merchant saw that the men were about to draw their swords. He said, "I have a solution."

The men fell silent and looked at him.

"Each head of the four families could hold a corner of the carpet," said the merchant. "That way, all four families would have the honour of carrying the carpet into the mosque."

The men looked at each other, then at the merchant. "Oh – we hadn't thought of that!" they said.

There and then, the merchant decided to go back home to his wife Salloma. She wasn't the stupidest person in the world, after all!

Hasan and the Golden Feather

Once there was a king who had two wives. The first wife gave him a son named Hasan, who grew up to be brave and handsome.

The second wife had two sons, and she wanted one of them to inherit the kingdom. So she said to her elder son, "Go and ask your father to make you heir to the throne."

But when he asked, the king replied, "If you want to be king, go and do something worthwhile, as I have done."

The second wife wasn't very happy with this, so she sent her younger son with the same request. But the king gave the same answer: "Go and do something worthwhile, as I have done."

Hearing what the second wife was up to, the first wife said to Hasan, "Your brothers have asked your father to make one of them heir to the throne. But you are his firstborn. Go and ask him to make you his heir."

Hasan went to his father, kissed his hand and

asked what his brothers had asked. But his father gave Hasan the same answer he had given them.

When Hasan told his mother, she said, "Then you must earn your right to the throne."

"But where shall I go, and what shall I do?" asked Hasan.

His mother thought for a moment. "Go on a quest, explore distant lands, and bring back something worthy of the heir to the throne."

✢ ✢ ✢

Hasan prepared himself for his long journey. Just as he was leaving, his mother said, "Come with me," and she took him to an olive grove. Standing in front of an ancient olive tree, she touched the trunk and said some words in a strange language.

All at once the tree shook violently, its trunk split open and out sprang a white horse!

Hasan stood there speechless.

The horse spoke: "How can I be of service to my queen?"

"Ballan, my faithful servant," said the queen. "This is my son Hasan. He is going on a quest. Take good care of him."

She turned to Hasan, kissed him goodbye and

said, "Farewell, my beloved son. May God protect and guide you in whatever you do." And she hurried back to the palace, leaving Hasan open-mouthed beside the olive tree.

After a while the horse pawed the ground and said, "Are you going to stand there all night?" Hasan came to his senses, climbed up on the back of the horse – and Ballan flew up into the night sky.

As they travelled, the horse explained to Hasan, "Your mother is a queen of the Jinn. When she met your father, he too was on a quest. He was trapped in a ghoul's net. She rescued him, they fell in love, and she left behind her family and throne to marry him."

On they flew, until in the distance they saw a great sea.

"We have been flying for a long time," said the horse. "Let's rest here for a while." So they rested on the seashore, and as Hasan walked along the shoreline, he noticed something sparkling in the sand. It was a feather – but unlike any feather he had ever seen! This feather was gold and silver. When he turned it to the right it shone with a golden light, and when it faced left, it shone with a silvery glow.

He showed it to Ballan, who shook his white head and warned him, "You'll be sorry if you take it, and sorry if you don't."

So Hasan decided to take the feather back. What did he have to lose?

Next day they reached a city, and Hasan took a room in the khan, where travellers stayed.

❖ ❖ ❖

The city was at war, and the king had ordered that no lamps were allowed to be lit at night. The king went out at night and inspected the streets with his wazir to check that his order was being obeyed.

It happened that just as the king was walking past the khan, Hasan took the feather from his pocket and put it on the table. The feather sparkled and lit the room with a brilliant light.

Seeing the light, the king ordered his guards to arrest Hasan and bring him to the palace. He said angrily, "You have disobeyed my orders and put the city in danger. The penalty is death by the sword!"

"But, Your Majesty," protested Hasan, "I lit no lamp."

The king grew even angrier. "You are a traitor and a liar. I saw the light with my own eyes."

Hasan said, "The light you saw didn't come from a lamp. It came from my feather."

"Nonsense!" said the king. "Feathers don't make light – they are just feathers. Again you lie." And he called to the guard, "Off with the traitor's head!"

But as Hasan was dragged off, he managed to pull the feather from his pocket. It fluttered on to the floor… and the room blazed as if it were lit with a hundred lamps!

The king was amazed. He held up the feather and turned it left and right.

"This is unbelievable. What an amazing feather!"

At that moment, the king's wazir whispered his ear, "Your Majesty, if a single feather shines like that, just imagine how the whole bird would look!"

The king thought for a moment, then said to Hasan, "I will pardon you – if you will bring me the bird whose feather this is. I will keep the feather with me until you return."

When Hasan told Ballan what had happened, the horse tossed his mane and said, "I told you you'll be sorry if you take it and sorry if you don't."

Hasan asked, "But what am I going to do now? And where can I find such a bird?"

Ballan said, "I know where the bird is, but first you must go to the king and tell him you need a cage made of gold and silver. And it must be a gift from the person closest to him."

✥ ✥ ✥

When Hasan told the king, he looked at his wazir and said, "That means you, my dear wazir."

A few days later the cage was ready, a wonder of beauty and craftsmanship. Hasan took the cage, jumped on Ballan's back and off they flew. After many days and many nights they arrived in a land of strange trees. Hasan had never seen anything like them. No two trees were alike. Each tree was taller than a hundred men standing on each other's heads, and each gleamed with different colours.

One tree was taller than the rest. Ballan whispered to Hasan, "Hang the cage on that tree with the door open, and hide yourself."

Moments later, a bird of dazzling beauty with shimmering gold and silver feathers flew into the tree. Her song was spellbinding: "What a beautiful cage," she sang, "just right for a glorious bird like me!"

Slowly she moved towards the cage, hopped inside – and Hasan snapped the door shut behind her.

Hasan took the bird back to the king, who was delighted – but his wazir was fuming, because he had had to pay for the cage.

"Your Majesty," said Hasan, "I have brought what you asked for. Now I would like a signed pardon and my feather back, please."

✤ ✤ ✤

The king was just about to give Hasan the feather, when an idea came to him.

"Not so fast, young man," he said, with a mischievous smile. "If the bird delights me so much, how much more would the bird's owner please me." And before Hasan could protest, the king said, "You have brought me the feather and the bird. Now bring me the bird's owner."

In desperation, Hasan went back to Ballan and told him of the king's command.

Ballan said, "You'll be sorry if you take it and sorry if you don't."

"But what shall I do?" said Hasan, "And where can I find the bird's owner?"

"I know where to find the owner," said the horse, "but first, go to the king and ask him to make you a boat of silver and gold. It must be so splendid that it will dazzle anyone who sees it. But it must be a gift from the person closest to the king."

Hasan smiled, and said, "I know – you mean the wazir."

Ballan said, "That will teach him not to put ideas into the king's head!"

A few weeks later the boat was ready, and Hasan and his horse set sail.

As they travelled, Ballan told him, "A princess owns the bird. She lives in a country seven seas away, in a castle guarded by ghouls and woven with magic spells. Anyone who tries to get near will be dead in an instant."

Hasan said, "Then how am I going to get in?"

"The only way," said Ballan, "is to make her come to you. You'll have to think of a way."

They reached the princess's kingdom and dropped anchor in a bay below the castle. Soon Hasan's wonderful boat became the talk of the land. People came from far and wide to see it, and news of the magical boat reached the princess. She pleaded with her father to let her see it, and eventually he agreed. So one evening, surrounded by her guards, she made her way down and asked Hasan to let her see the boat.

Hasan said, "You are welcome, Your Highness, but you will have to come alone. If your guards, with their heavy armour and weapons, step aboard, the boat will sink under their weight."

The princess was eager to see the boat, so she agreed. She wandered here and there, admiring the splendid carvings and exquisite furnishings, and did not notice that the boat was moving. When she went out on deck, she found to her dismay that she was at sea!

She pleaded with Hasan to take her back, but he refused.

Then she took off her ring and threw it into the sea.

During the long voyage back, Hasan told her about himself and she about herself. When they reached port, Hasan delivered the princess to the king.

Seeing her beauty, the king wanted to marry her straight away. But the princess refused, saying, "I will not marry you until you find the ring I lost at sea."

So once again, Hasan received a command – this time to find the princess's ring.

When Hasan told Ballan, the horse pawed the ground and said, "I told you: you'll be sorry if you take it and sorry if you don't."

Hassan said, "But how am I going to find a ring lying on the bottom of the sea?"

"I know how to find it," said Ballan, "but first, ask the king to give you a big ship filled with sacks of flour. And it must be a gift – from You-Know-Who…"

A few days later the ship was ready, and Hasan set sail into the seven seas.

When they reached a certain spot, Ballan asked Hasan to throw the entire cargo of flour into the sea.

Then they waited – and within hours, a huge fish

broke through the waves.

"I am King of the Fish. Who fed my subjects?" it gurgled.

"I did, Your Majesty," replied Hasan.

"You are exceedingly generous," said the Fish King. "How can I reward you?"

"Can you help me find a ring?" asked Hasan. "It was dropped in this spot, and sank to the bottom of the sea."

The Fish King disappeared under the water, and reappeared a few minutes later with the ring in his mouth.

Hasan sailed back and gave the ring to the king.

But the princess still refused to marry the king, saying, "I cannot marry you until you fetch my horse."

Once again the king commanded Hasan, and Hasan went back to Ballan, who said, "You'll be sorry if you take it, and sorry if you don't."

"But what shall I do?" said Hasan, "And where can I find the princess's horse?"

Ballan replied, "I know where the horse is. But first, go to the king and ask him to make a saddle made of gold and a harness of silver. And of course, it must be a gift."

Soon the saddle and harness were ready, and Ballan told Hasan, "When we find the princess's horse, you'll have to approach him carefully. If his eyes are open, he will be asleep, and you can tie him with the harness and saddle him. But if his eyes are closed, don't go near him – he will tear you apart!"

For days and nights they travelled, until they saw below them a barren hill with only one tree. A black stallion was standing nearby. They landed on the hill. Cautiously Hasan approached the horse and saw that his eyes were open, so he came closer and tied him with the silver harness, then saddled and mounted the horse. The stallion flew up into the air. During the day they travelled, and at night Hasan tied him to a tree, until finally he reached the king's palace.

The princess smiled happily when she saw her horse. She stood beside him talking softly and stroking his mane – then suddenly jumped on his back and flew away!

Hasan mounted Ballan and tried to catch up with her. It wasn't until a few days later that he found her, sitting in the shadow of a tree.

"Why did you run away?" he asked.

The princess said sadly, "I can't marry a man who ordered my kidnapping, and who is as old as my father. Besides, I don't love him."

Hasan's heart leapt, for ever since their voyage in the gold and silver boat he had been secretly in love with the princess.

"Will you marry me?" he asked.

The princess smiled. "Yes, of course!" she said, "but on one condition. We must go back to my country and get my father's blessing."

So Hasan and the princess travelled back to her country, where they were married, and her father loaded his daughter with gifts to take to her new home.

Then Hasan set off home with his bride.

His mother had almost given up hope of seeing her son again, and welcomed him with delight.

As for the king, when he saw Hasan, he asked him, "Well, how was your quest? Did you find something worthy of the throne?"

Hasan replied, "Yes. I found a good wife, the best any man could want."

Hearing this, the king's heart overflowed with pride and joy – and then and there he declared Hasan his heir.

As for the king's wazir, he left the country in disgust!

Sources

Ghaddar the Ghoul
Adapted and retold from *Kan Ya ma Kan: Popular stories from Jerusalem*, Rushdi Al Ashhab (Alloush Publishers, Jerusalem, 1996).

The Farmer who Followed his Dream
Retold from versions heard since childhood. A version can be found in *The Book of the Thousand Nights and a Night*, translated into English by Richard F. Burton (London: The Burton Club, 1885).

Dancing Jasmine, Singing Water
Adapted and retold from *Kan Ya ma Kan: Popular stories from Jerusalem*, Rushdi Al Ashhab (Alloush Publishers, Jerusalem, 1996).

Tanbouri's Clown
Told to me at bedtime by my mother. The original story can be found, untitled, in *The Thousand and One Nights*. My version was written with Rasha Hammami, first in English rhyme, then published in Arabic (Tamer Institute, Ramallah, 1996).

How Swallow Tricked Snake
Collected in the Jenin area, entitled *Why snakes eat frogs, why swallow has a fork in his tail and why mosquitoes can't sing*. My version was written with Rasha Hammami, first in English rhyme, then published in Arabic (Tamer Institute, Ramallah, 1996).

I Landed at the Prince's Party
Heard in Jenin and Tulkarm, in different versions. Another version can be found in *Kan Ya ma Kan: Popular stories from Jerusalem*, Rushdi Al Ashhab (Alloush Publishers, Jerusalem, 1996). My version was published in Arabic under a title which translates as 'A story that begins and ends with lies' (Tamer Institute, Ramallah, 2003).

Hungry Wolf and Crafty Fox
Retold from an oral retelling heard in the village of Zababdah, near Jenin. Zababdah is a Christian village, hence the reference to the Cross.

Stupid Salma
Retold from versions heard since childhood.

Hasan and the Golden Feather
Retold from a story entitled 'Bushel of Gold' in the collection *Speak, bird, speak again: Palestinian Arab Folktales*, Sharif Kana'anah and Ibrahim Mohawi (University of California Press, 1992).